The Kitten Book

For Roxanna and Jeremy

The author warmly thanks
Jackie and Lupin Lawson for making
this book possible.

First U.S. edition 1992
First published in Great Britain in 1991 by Walker Books Ltd., London.

ISBN 1-56402-020-7

Library of Congress Catalog Card Number 91-71841
Library of Congress Cataloging-in-Publication information is available.

10 9 8 7 6 5 4 3 2 1

Printed and bound in Hong Kong by
Dai Nippon (Pte.) Ltd.

Candlewick Press
2067 Massachusetts Avenue
Cambridge, Massachusetts 02140

The
Kitten Book

—by Camilla Jessel—

CANDLEWICK PRESS
CAMBRIDGE, MASSACHUSETTS

L̲upin the Burmese cat is about to have kittens. Nine weeks ago she was mated with a tomcat called Tango, after which several tiny kittens began to grow inside her. At first each one was smaller than the point of a pin, but now they are large and strong enough to be born.

Lupin's mistress has prepared a special heated bed with a soft blanket and a roof to keep the draft off the newborn kittens. But Lupin prowls around the house, searching for a more secret nesting place.

Where can she be? At last she is found high up in the kitchen – not a safe place for kittens to be born! She disappears again, trying out every cupboard and cranny upstairs and downstairs. In the end she decides the cat bed will be best.

She stretches herself comfortably on top of the blanket, ready to give birth.

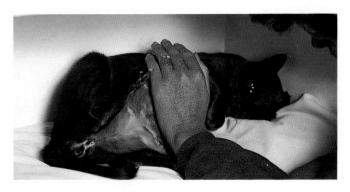

Before the kittens are born, they lie
warm and snug inside their mother's
womb, each protected by its own watery
bubble. They emerge one at a time.
Lupin has to use her inner muscles to
push them out along her birth passage.

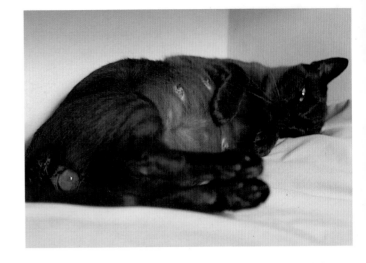

Kandy, the first kitten, is born at ten
thirty-five that night.

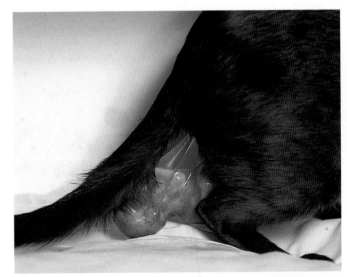

Lupin knows by instinct that she must
lick away the skin of the bubble so that
Kandy can start to breathe.

Lupin's tongue works its way very gently all over her baby – mouth, nose, eyes, ears, tail, paws.

Each of Kandy's tiny claws has a soft cover to prevent it from scratching the mother cat while the kitten is being born, and Lupin licks these away too. Soon Kandy is perfectly clean.

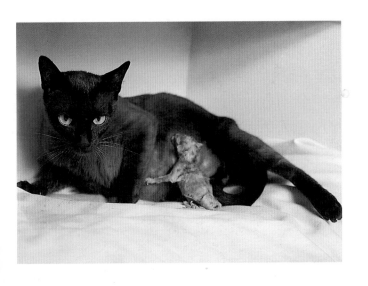

Kandy cannot see or hear anything yet, and she wriggles along rather than walks. However, her sensitive nose and whiskers help her to feel where she is and find the right place for her first drink of warm milk from her mother. Lupin is quietly purring. Even Kandy makes a tiny, faint rumble of a purr.

The second kitten, Brandy, is born just after eleven o'clock.

After another twenty minutes the third one, Shandy, appears. Then Mandy, Andy, and Sandy.

Two females, four males! Most cats have three, four, or five kittens. Lupin is very busy licking her babies clean and nudging them into place so that they can suckle.

It is two o'clock in the morning. All the kittens are asleep or feeding. Lupin's mistress brings her a bowl of warm milk, egg yolk, and honey to give the mother cat some extra strength.

Then she changes the bedding and settles the new family comfortably for the night.

Time now to turn off the light and leave them peacefully snuggled together.

But what is this? Another kitten is arriving in its wet little bubble onto the warm, clean, dry sheet!

Kitten number seven looks like a miniature lion with a bright pink nose. He is called Dandy.

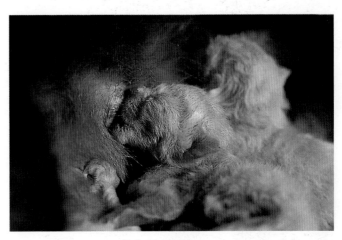

By three o'clock in the morning Dandy is warm and dry and curled up with his brothers and sisters. Because their stomachs are very small, the kittens wake up and feed every hour or two, so Lupin cannot get much rest. But she doesn't seem to mind. She keeps purring and purring.

All the kittens remain blind and deaf for a while.

At six days Dandy's eyes are just beginning to open. He can tell the difference between bright light and darkness but cannot see his mother or the other kittens yet.

At two weeks although his eyes are bright, Dandy still can see only hazily. His ears are opening out too, and he jumps at loud noises.

By three weeks he can at last see and hear quite well.

It also takes a while for the strength of Dandy's legs to develop. At first they are too floppy to walk, so he slithers along on his stomach, using his paws like paddles.

At ten days although his legs are stronger, they still bend under his weight, and it is difficult for him to move around.

Until the kittens can walk properly, Lupin has to carry them around in her mouth if she wants to move the nest.

Even at one month their legs hardly lift their bodies off the ground.

At five weeks they are still not very good at walking, sometimes going sideways while aiming straight ahead.

For the first three weeks the kittens just sleep and feed.

Their fur is still thin, so they can easily catch cold. When their mother leaves them so that she can eat her dinner, they pile up together for warmth.

Lupin never goes far from her babies. She has a strong instinct to guard them from danger. She is even suspicious of Julie, an old friend from next door.

Julie knows how to hold Brandy so that he feels safe and supported. However, the kittens do not enjoy being cuddled at this early stage. They are instinctively frightened of strangers. Dandy already hisses at someone he doesn't know.

When they are three or four weeks old, the kittens begin to enjoy human company. Even then, Julie knows that she will have to be extremely gentle and careful.

Compared with human babies, kittens grow very fast. A baby takes six months to double its birth weight, but a kitten takes only one week!

Kittens feed every two or three hours, sucking at their mother's teats and pumping with their paws to help the milk flow quickly. By the time they are four weeks old, they have doubled their size again, and Lupin is almost invisible at feeding times!

Soon the kittens will need solid food as well as milk.

1 day old

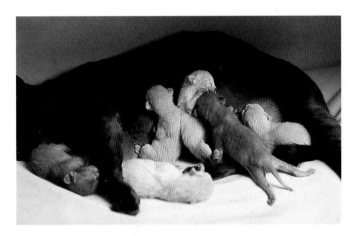

10 days old

28 days old

At first Dandy does not think much of solid food, but soon he realizes that chopped chicken and minced fish are delicious.

For a while Dandy needs only a small amount of food a day. He swallows quite well, although he still has very few teeth.

Dandy, Kandy, Brandy, Sandy, Mandy, Andy, and Shandy are always well washed by their mother after meals. From the start, she has kept the kittens beautifully sweet-smelling and tidy. Like all cat mothers, she eats their messes, never letting them fall into their nesting bed.

Cats are the cleanest of animals, and they never make their houses dirty. Already at three weeks Dandy, copying his mother, can use the litter box, carefully scrabbling the litter to cover his droppings.

Brandy is the first to wash himself.

The kittens have to learn to sit up before they can practice lifting one paw for cleaning. It is difficult to balance at first, and they sometimes fall over.

Dandy's problem is that his paw keeps sliding off his nose before his tongue can reach it!

At one month the kittens spend much of the day playing. They are not just having fun. Through their games they are gaining experience and practicing survival skills they will need for their grown-up life.

Dandy learns by exploring everything he sees. He almost scalds his nose when he sniffs a cup of tea, and this teaches him to avoid hot things.

At this stage the only drink he needs is his mother's milk, but he is already finding out about water, which will soon be essential for him.

In ancient times cats were tree animals, so Dandy has the instinct to climb. His climbing games help him to become more and more skillful and safe.

He needs to learn to balance, and he practices again and again until he can stay on the chair rung.

Cats living in the wild are brave and clever at killing dangerous creatures, such as rats and snakes. Also, sometimes adult cats fight each other quite ferociously. Because they have slippery fur and loose skin, it is difficult for other animals to wound cats, although cats' ears often get bitten during fights.

So kittens, even those reared in a warm, comfortable house, instinctively practice fighting, stalking, pouncing, and jumping to help them get ready for adult life. At first their fighting games are quite gentle, but they get rougher and rougher.

The kittens also like to have pretend fights with their mother's tail. Lupin swishes it around very fast, teasing the kittens until they become quick enough to catch it.

The kittens do not use their claws on one another, however, and they do not get hurt. Their fighting games help them to become quick and clever in their reactions, and to develop their natural courage.

For the first five weeks the kittens stay in the room where they were born. Though the door is wide open, they play close to their nesting bed. All kittens have this instinct to stay inside their own territory; it would be a matter of life or death for kittens growing up in the wild.

Dandy is the first to explore farther afield. It is very exciting trying to climb the stairs. But suddenly he feels lost. "Meow, meow!"

Soon all the kittens are courageous enough to explore new territory. The stairs are the very best place for a game. Now the whole house is theirs to discover. Everything they find, they examine with their noses, paws, and teeth.

The kittens become more and more mischievous.

Dandy tries his paws at knitting!

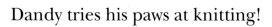

As the kittens grow, they play more and more energetically. They are no longer fluffy little bundles; their bodies have become sleek, sinewy, and strong. They can stretch and balance, pounce and leap into the air, almost like full-grown cats.

For their first three months the kittens have to stay indoors. Neighborhood cats who visit the garden could pass on germs that could make the kittens ill.

At nine weeks, then again at twelve weeks, the vet vaccinates them against disease.

After their second injection the kittens are allowed outside. Dandy is scared at first.

He finds a safe place from which to look around. Brandy is braver – he is soon investigating interesting new toys.

A few days later Dandy seems to be the bravest. He climbs very high and leaps into the garden next door. He then sets off to explore.

The tomatoes smell peculiar . . .

and some strange, scary creatures do not answer when he meows to them.

Dandy suddenly wants to be back home with his brothers and sisters, but the fence is too steep and slippery to climb from this side, and the tree leads nowhere.

He meows loudly, but no one hears him.

Luckily the next-door neighbor soon comes home from work. She brings Dandy back to his family.

Lupin gives Dandy a good washing.

Then she lets him take a comforting drink. The kittens do not really need their mother's milk anymore. They already eat grown-up cat food and drink plenty of water. But Lupin still likes to mother them from time to time.

However, they are ready now to go to their new homes.

First Kandy goes, then Shandy and Sandy.

When Thomas and Vicky come to choose a kitten, their mother suggests that they find the quietest of the brood, who will be cuddly and good and not too much trouble.

Andy is purring in his sleep; at first they think he is the sweetest.

Then Brandy wakes up – he is adorable! They are just about to choose him when they hear a lot of scuffling behind them. What has Dandy found?

From then on, Thomas and Vicky lose interest in the other kittens. They decide that a naughty, lively kitten will be much more fun than a sleepy one. Dandy likes the children too. He wants them to play with him.

But he is not at all pleased when they put him in the cat carrier for the journey.

Thomas and Vicky long to cuddle Dandy on the long drive, but they know it is safer for him to stay in the carrier.

At last they are home.

But for Dandy it's not home. It is a strange new frightening place.

He jumps out of Thomas's arms and tucks himself behind the toy box. "Just let him look around and get used to everything," says the children's mother.

While Dandy peeps out shyly, Thomas and Vicky carefully arrange the blanket on Dandy's new bed. They talk softly to him. "Look, there's your litter box, and here's your water bowl," says Thomas. "They'll always be in the same place so that you know where to find them."

"And here's your delicious dinner," says Vicky. "It's scrumptious chopped chicken with juicy gravy. Why don't you come out and have a little taste?"

The children wait and wait, quietly watching while Dandy watches them. Then Thomas has an idea. He makes a pretend mouse and tries swinging it gently up and down. At first nothing happens. Dandy *wants* to play, but he is still frightened.

Thomas is very patient, and in the end Dandy cannot resist the game.

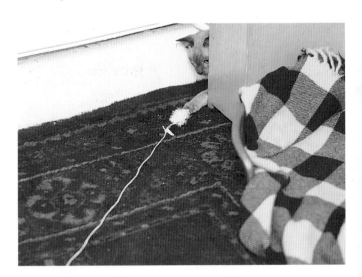

After he has played for a few minutes, he sits down and gives himself a good washing.

"That's a very good sign," says Vicky. "It means he's beginning to feel at home."

Soon Dandy is feeling confident enough to look around his new house. But someone has left the back door open; the kitten rushes into the garden. The children run after him. They are frightened that he will escape over the fence to try to find his way to his old home, getting lost or run over on the way.

Dandy does not want to be caught. He hides . . .

. . . but when Thomas comes close, he rushes up a tree, climbing higher and higher.

Suddenly he is stuck, and he meows pathetically for help. "Oh, I wish we had a ladder," says Vicky. "What can we do?"

Their mother is just coming out with a stool when Dandy finds his own way out of the tree.

The children are terrified that he will be hurt, but they don't need to worry. Cats always manage to land on their feet.

After that they are very careful to keep Dandy indoors until he is absolutely settled in their house.

Meanwhile he is busy taking over the household. He explores each room, sniffing everything, brushing against each object as if to say, "Now it's mine!" and pawing it to see if it jumps.

It is easy to train a dog, but cats expect their humans to obey them! Dandy thinks that they should play with him and stroke him whenever he likes and share their fish with him. Thomas is strict: he puts Dandy back on the floor, but Dandy soon jumps up again.

They have to cuddle Dandy just the right way. When Thomas holds him too tightly, even by mistake, Dandy kicks out fiercely with his sharp claws.

He enjoys being held very gently, but only when he is in the mood. Vicky and Thomas realize that they cannot treat him like a toy – they have to consider his feelings just as if he were another person.

It does not take Dandy long to train his family. He, in turn, is nearly always good.

And of course they have wonderful games together.

The only problem is that Dandy keeps getting lost. It is difficult to see him when he is fast asleep in Mom's briefcase. He becomes visible only when he wakes up.

Wherever Dandy sleeps, his hungry stomach acts like an alarm clock, reminding him when it is time for his supper. If he does not appear, then it means he is in trouble – like the day he is trapped in the clothes cupboard. But then he tells the children where he is with deep, moany meows.

One evening Dandy fails to come for his supper. It is late. It is dark. The children search everywhere. There is no sound from him, no sign at all that he is anywhere in the house.

"He's lost forever!" says Vicky. She is just about to burst into tears – when all of a sudden Thomas sees him…

Now Dandy *really* feels at home!